BEAR HUGS

BEAR HUGS

Kate Tym
Illustrated by John Blackman

SCHOLASTIC INC.

New York Toronto London Auckland Sydney
Mexico City New Delhi Hong Kong

For Mandy, Martin and Jo—friends in need . . .

ISBN 0-439-26234-8

12 11 10 9 8 7 6 5 4 3   1 2 3 4 5/0

Printed in the U.S.A.   40

First Scholastic printing, January 2001

Cover design by Mandy Sherliker.
Typeset by Dorchester Typesetting Group Ltd.

Introduction

I've always been a big fan of bears. I sleep with my teddy, I take my little bear, Winston, with me whenever I travel anywhere and I'm Winnie-the-Pooh's number one fan! But in writing *Bear Hugs* I've discovered a whole lot more about these majestic creatures and their other wild friends. Many cultures throughout the world have long known what impressive and soulful animals bears are and it would pay the human race now to remember such things, stop destroying their natural habitat and learn to treat them with the respect they deserve. On vacation in Nepal last year I actually saw three bears in the wild. They were Sloth Bears and lived in a carefully guarded national park. They were amazing! Dark, dark brown with shaggy fur and enormous behinds, it was hard to imagine that anything so cute and cuddly-looking contained such an awesome amount of power. And sad to think that the only way these incredible creatures are able to survive is when they're fenced in with an armed guard surrounding them twenty-four hours a day. But, it's not all bad news! There are plenty of people out there working very hard for bears and their pals and fighting to ensure that even in a hundred years from now, all animals will still have a piece of the Earth to call their own. So let's all celebrate bears, after all . . . they're just grrrrreat!

Kate Tym

Bears are everywhere!

Bears are found in most parts of the world, though in many countries they are now scarce and rarely found outside the large game reservations. They live in widely different climatic regions; the huge white Polar Bears live in Arctic regions; the Black and Brown Bears in the temperate zones; while in tropical countries are the oriental Sloth Bears and the Spectacled Bears. Those that live in cold climates hibernate through the winter. Bears belong to the Order of Carnivora; flesh-eaters, but in fact they eat a rich variety of food – even the large Brown Bears eat great quantities of fruit and vegetables – and spend much of their time tearing to pieces old logs and digging in the ground in order to find grubs, worms, and insects. The female generally has a litter of two or three cubs, which are at first extremely small – Polar Bear cubs are only about 12 inches long at birth!

7

Polar Bears

These are among the largest of the bears, often being nearly 10 feet long. They're lucky enough to even have hair on the soles of their feet, which gives them a good grip on the slippery ice they live on. When hungry, they're really best avoided, as they might take one look at you and think "here comes dinner!" In the winter they eat seals and walruses and lots of fish too; but in summer they have a mainly vegetable diet. In the fall the female Polar Bear, having fed well and laid up a good stock of fat, retires to a cave beneath the snow and gives birth to her cubs in mid-winter. Polar Bears show a strong love for their babies and when conditions are bad and they're feeling a bit on the hungry side, a mother bear has even been known to divide what little food she's found between her two cubs and only take a tiny little bit of food to eat herself.

Giggly Bear

What do you get if you cross an owl with a skunk?

A bird that smells but who doesn't give a hoot!

Brown Bears

These are found in a few places in western and in most of eastern Europe, and in Asia and North America, their size and the shade of their coats varying according to where they live. In Alaska there are Brown Bears, called Kodiaks, which are sometimes as much as 10 feet long, and weigh over 1,500 pounds! They are the largest of all the bears.

The Grizzly Bear of the Rocky Mountains is another huge animal and immensely strong. Although such enormous creatures, these giant brown bears are actually fairly timid and they really only turn nasty if they feel threatened or cornered or are wounded or trying to protect their young. Otherwise they will generally do their best to try to avoid any contact with human kind – but don't try putting them to the test, whatever you do! Once angered, Grizzly and Alaskan Bears are very dangerous creatures indeed. Grizzlies are protected in the National Parks of the USA and Canada which is a good thing, as elsewhere they have become almost extinct.

Black Bears

The American Black Bear is a much smaller animal than the big Brown Bear and is still to be found in many parts of Canada and the United States. It is in fact now a protected animal. In the Yellowstone Park in the USA Black Bears sometimes hold up cars to beg for food, and, if not given any, they have been known in their anger to try to tear the car to pieces! They rarely kill wild animals, but often attack sheep and raid farmyards. They usually make their winter dens under the upturned roots of a fallen tree or beneath a pile of logs. They scrape together a few bushes or leaves to make a bed, and wait for the first snowstorm to complete the roof and fill in the remaining chinks.

There are Black Bears in Asia – from Iran, right through to the Himalayas and China. There is also a smaller species in Japan. They live in the mountains or forests, where they climb the trees in search of fruit. In Malaysia you will find small Honey Bears or Sun Bears, which have short, sleek, black coats. They, too, are excellent climbers and in their search for honey are very clever at finding bees' nests, and almost as clever at managing not to get stung!

Bears of the world

1. Polar Bear
Found in Arctic regions of
Canada, Greenland,
Norway, Russia and USA.
Between 21,000 and 28,000
left in the wild.
VULNERABLE

**2. American
Black Bear**
Found on North
American
continent.
Less than 700,000
left in the wild.

3. Brown Bear
Found in North
America
("Grizzly"), Asia
and Europe.
Less than 180,000
left in the wild.

4. Spectacled Bear
Found on South
American
continent.
Approx. 10,000 left
in the wild.
VULNERABLE

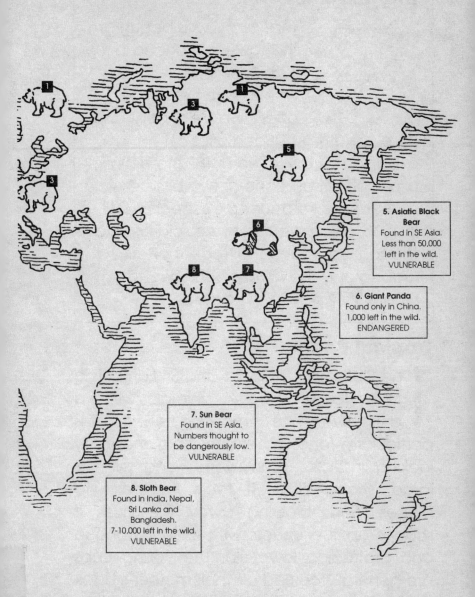

5. Asiatic Black Bear
Found in SE Asia.
Less than 50,000
left in the wild.
VULNERABLE

6. Giant Panda
Found only in China.
1,000 left in the wild.
ENDANGERED

7. Sun Bear
Found in SE Asia.
Numbers thought to
be dangerously low.
VULNERABLE

8. Sloth Bear
Found in India, Nepal,
Sri Lanka and
Bangladesh.
7-10,000 left in the wild.
VULNERABLE

Did you know...?

That a zoo was begun at the Tower of London in 1235 with three leopards which were joined soon after by a polar bear and an elephant. After centuries of expansion, it dwindled in 1822 to a bear, an elephant and one or two birds. A new keeper introduced 59 species until, in 1835, a lion mauled some soldiers and the zoo was moved to Regent's Park, leaving only the ravens behind . . . where they stay to this day.

Tropical Bears

The Sloth Bear of India and Sri Lanka is a fairly large shaggy animal, with a distinctive white V mark on its chest. It is particularly fond of termites (big maggoty looking insects – yum yum!) and with its large, strong claws it tears the nests to pieces then, blowing away the dust, it scoops up the insects with its long tongue and protruding lower lip. The young cubs are generally carried on their mother's back when the animals are on the move; it's a funny sight to watch them dismount at the feeding ground and scramble back to their seats at the first alarm.

The only bear to be found in South America is the Spectacled Bear, which lives in the mountains of Peru and Colombia. It is a small inoffensive black

Did you know...?

Inuit people believe that bears are supreme beings and that if they overhear a human conversation, they will know if they are being talked about. To avoid such embarrassment, the Inuit often refer to the bear as *pissitog* or "the walker" so that even if he hears them, he won't know it's him they're gassing about – pretty sneaky, I think you'll agree!

bear, with a white breast and pale-colored rings round its eyes, which give it a clownish appearance. It lives in remote areas, and avoids man as much as possible. It's a real veg-head, happy to chow down on a diet of fruit and vegetables.

Panda Bears

For a long time, the world of science couldn't decide if a Panda actually was a bear or not! It remained unclassified until 1980 when finally it was allowed bear status, due to progress made in the field of molecular biology. Before that it was considered to be a distant relative both of the bear and of the raccoon! Pandas inhabit the mountain regions of China. They are solitary creatures and barely even pay any attention to each other, until it's time to mate! They live on a diet mostly made up of bamboo, with other plants thrown in for variety and possibly the odd rabbit not smart enough to get out of the panda's way! Pandas appear very slothful, spending around twelve to sixteen hours a day eating . . . well, I suppose there are worse ways you could spend your time. Sadly, there are only around 1,000 pandas left in the wild and their existence continues to be threatened by the destruction of their habitat and, I'm sorry to say, poaching, that goes on despite the fact that pandas are also now a protected species.

Giggly Bear

Shopper: *I'd like a pair of crocodile shoes please.*

Assistant: *Certainly madam – what size does the crocodile take?*

Koala Bears

Uh – sorry guys, I hate to tell you this, but koala bears aren't really bears at all – they're marsupials! An animal is classed as a marsupial if it carries its young in a pouch; a kangaroo does this, and so does a koala – so it's officially *not* a bear at all. But who cares – it looks pretty bear-ish and it's absolutely cute, cuddly and completely adorable. Koala means "no drink" in the language of the aboriginal people native to Australia. Koalas do drink, but not very often and not very much; they can't really be bothered to come down from their perches in the Eucalyptus trees for long enough. Koala young – known as joeys – live in their mother's pouch for the first six months of life and then spend the next six months riding on her back, clinging on as best they can as Mom ambles around in the trees. Koalas can live to be around 17 years old. Today, there are probably no more than 30,000 koalas left, which may sound a lot . . . but, sadly, isn't.

Giggly Bear

What's the difference between a coyote and a flea?

One howls on the prairie, the other prowls on the hairy!

Having a Roaring Time

Fourteen-year-old Gary MacCammick has a very unusual friend – a lion called Nahla! Gary's grandfather Ellis Daw and his wife Lynne run the Dartmoor Wildlife Park in Devon, UK and have Gary as a regular visitor. It was during one of these visits that Nahla and her three siblings were born. But the cub's mother, Peggy, had trouble accepting her four new arrivals and sadly three of the cubs died. Only Nahla survived, and was lovingly hand-reared by her new human "family." She soon accepted Ellis as her father, Lynne as her mother and Gary as her rather boisterous brother.

As a baby Nahla easily fitted into the palm of Gary's hand and the cute little bundle of fur soon stole his heart. At ten months Nahla's not nearly as little, she eats over eight pounds of red meat a day, and weighing in at just over 112 pounds of solid muscle she's even heavier than Gary is! But that doesn't stop them having fun together.

Gary takes Nahla for walks on a lead round the park; Nahla also loves a quick game of soccer and they like to have the odd wrestle together. Nahla regards Gary as a brother and a bit of rough and tumble is great fun between a pair of excitable young lion cubs!

Soon Gary and Nahla will have to part; she is turning into a very big cat and will be going to live at another wildlife park but Gary will never forget the love he shared with his "sister" Nahla the lion.

★ *Celebrity Bear* ★
Baloo

The Indian word for bear is . . . Baloo! And that's where we find this particular bear, deep in the Indian jungle looking after the man-cub Mowgli. Taken from *The Jungle Book* by Rudyard Kipling, Walt Disney immortalized Baloo as a smooth talking, jazz-loving softy with a bit more brawn than brains.

Snake in the grass

In 1999 two US expeditions were launched in

Ecuador to search in the Amazon for the world's largest snake. The snake is a 30-foot-long anaconda. One of the ways of catching the slippery critter is to wade into the water and have a feel around for it! Nice job!

Giggly Bear

What *do* you get if you cross a hippo with a kangaroo?

A hoppypotamus.

It's a Wrap

At the Sea Life Center in Portsmouth, UK, a blind shark has been put in a padded tank to stop him damaging his nose. Pugh the 3-foot-long dogfish couldn't see the glass of his tank and kept hitting his poor old nose against it. When Pugh first arrived at the center, having been brought there by a kindly fisherman, he was very thin but staff didn't realize he was blind. However, when they noticed that he kept hitting the sides of the tank and didn't seem to have any awareness of where they were, it soon became apparent that poor Pugh couldn't see. The next step was to make his environment nice and safe for him, so they got out the bubble-wrap and lined his tank with it. Hey-presto! – his very own safe and sound padded cell. Pugh's now doing very well, and despite having a slightly unusually shaped head and a look on his face like he's always squinting, everyone seems to agree he's really very sweet and they wouldn't want to change him for the world!

Did you know...?

If sharks stop moving they sink! Sounds like they need swimming lessons to me!

Tales from the ABC

There are a number of stories scattered throughout this book which were all sent to me by Daryl Ratajczak the Curator of the Appalachian Bear Center (ABC). This is a wonderful organization responsible for

 rehabilitating and releasing bears that have either had accidents or (particularly cubs) lost their mothers. Set in the beautiful countryside just outside the Great Smoky Mountain National Park in Tennessee, it's right in the heart of bear country and provides a unique and wonderful service caring for any bears that need their help in that area. Run almost exclusively on the help of volunteers, it is a charitable organization in constant need of funds to help it keep up its amazing work.

If you would like more information, or to send a donation, you can contact the Appalachian Bear Center at the following address:

Daryl Ratajczak
Appalachian Bear Center
P.O. Box 364
Townsend, TN 37882

Phone: (423) 448-0143
www.appbears.org

Cat and Mouse Games

A cat in Thailand called Ouan has a very unusual pal – Tua-Lek the mouse! Ouan's owner Jaranai Nanongtoom, is a roadside coffee seller in Phichit, North Thailand and he's become used to the loving relationship his cat has with his little squeaky friend. From the day Tua-Lek first emerged from a paddy field Ouan has treated the little mouse like a kitten. Ouan looks out for Tua-Lek and is very protective of him. What's more they play and explore together, share the same bowl and when it's time for a nap they even cuddle up together and Tua-Lek lets Ouan give her a nice wash with her tongue. Jaranai is a Buddhist and he's a firm believer that the two must have been very good friends in a previous life. Well, one thing's for certain, even if they weren't friends in a previous life, they certainly are now!

Panda Pal

In April 1996 Gu Yingming, a Chinese farmer, had a very special guest to stay . . . a giant panda! The family rather liked their cuddly visitor and named him Maomao. They were so delighted with their guest that they made sure he had all the home comforts he could need and gave him plenty of bamboo shoots and honey to keep him going. Maomao was so happy that he stayed with Gu Yingming and his family for four whole days. The family think he would have stayed longer, but they made the mistake of feeding him on some meat which, being mainly vegetarian, didn't agree with poor Maomao's tummy. Animal protection staff took over and Maomao went off to recuperate and suddenly, having been full of big black-and-white bear, Gu Yingming's house felt very empty indeed!

Short Stuff

A baby giraffe at Chester Zoo in the UK had to be hand-reared by its keepers – at $6\frac{1}{2}$ feet tall it was a bit on the short side to be fed comfortably by its mother. It towered over most of its keepers and they had a real stretch on their hands when it was time for the bottle – but they didn't mind, it was worth it to see the giraffe grow up big and strong and hopefully, one day, it'll be almost as tall as its mother!

Giggly Bear

What's big, gray, and mutters?

A mumbo jumbo!

The "Koala" Legend

There was once an orphaned boy called Koobor. He was made to feel very unwanted by the rest of his family. They neglected him badly. One of the main things they kept from him was water – poor Koobor was always thirsty and never had enough to drink. Every morning when his relatives went off to forage for food they would leave him behind but, before they went, they always made sure that they hid any water they had stored away from him. But one morning, they forgot. Koobor seized his chance and went to get the buckets of water. He found a Eucalyptus tree and hung the buckets from all of its branches.

Koobor was quite a special boy with a certain amount of magic about him so, when he climbed into the tree and sang a special song, the tree grew at an incredible rate and quite quickly towered above all others in the forest.

Eventually Koobor's family returned. They were angry that they'd been so careless and left the water within Koobor's sights. When they saw Koobor high in the tree with all their water, they were hopping mad! They yelled at him to bring the water down but Koobor, who'd gone thirsty for so long, refused. It was time for them to have a taste of their own medicine.

Koobor's family kept trying to get him down from the tree and eventually they succeeded, only to beat him badly as soon as his feet hit the ground. Koobor lay, bloody and battered but, as his family watched in amazement, they saw his body heal itself and rearrange itself into the shape of a koala, which clambered back up into its tree where it would be happy to live with virtually no water at all for the rest of its days.

Did you know...?

That a teddy bear accompanied the first men to walk on the moon in July 1969? One small step for a teddy, one giant leap for mankind!

Cherokee

On October 3, 1997, Daryl Ratajczak received a call from Doug Scott of the Tennessee Wildlife Resources Agency. He told Daryl of a cub that had been hit by a car on Cherokee Road in Washington County. The cub was fine but very sadly, had lost its mother and the Appalachian Bear Center would be the ideal place to care for the little cub until it was ready to go back to the wild. Daryl was happy to take the cub, little knowing that over the next two months the ABC would get thirteen similar calls!

Since this was the first cub of their fall season, the people at the ABC were anxious to get things under way. The necessary paperwork was filled out and as much background information as possible was found on the new cub. It seemed that Cherokee – as he was named – had pressed his luck by trying to cross Cherokee Road during the hours of daylight. Crossing a busy road in the middle of the day is not the smartest thing a bear cub can do and, unluckily for Cherokee, before he'd even made it half way across he'd been hit by a speeding car and knocked unconscious into a nearby drainage ditch. Thankfully, a couple of motorists saw what had happened and pulled over to lend a hand. They loaded up the unconscious cub into the back of a pickup truck and began driving to the nearest Veterinary Hospital.

Richard Shelton, of Limestone, Tennessee, was the lucky one who got the job of watching over the 19 pound cub while his friend did the driving. The small cub was breathing regularly and did not appear to have sustained any major injuries, so the pair felt quite confident that he might be OK if they could get him to the right people quite quickly. But, what they hadn't really counted on was . . . the cub waking up!

Within a few minutes of setting off on their journey, the bear was regaining his senses so Mr. Shelton did the first thing that came into his head and simply grabbed the cub and held on for dear life! Luckily they made it to the Veterinary Hospital but the hard part was yet to come . . . letting go of a very strong, wound up, little cub was not going to be easy! But, despite the commotion that followed, the vets were eventually able to give the bear a checkup and a clean bill of health. But, not before "Cherokee" gave Mr. Shelton a handshake in the only way he knew how – with his teeth. Ouch!

Luckily "Cherokee" was fine and after a fourteen week stay at the bear center, he was released into Cherokee National Forest weighing over 70 pounds! Although there was a happy ending to this story, please DO NOT attempt to handle any injured bears you may come across. Instead, telephone your nearest Wildlife Resources and let them deal with the problem – after all they're used to it and they'll know just what to do to make everything good and safe for you . . . and for the bear too!

Giggly Bear

What do you give to a rabbit who feels faint?

Hare restorer!

The Wise Old Man

In Aboriginal myth, the Koala is said to embody the Wise Old Man, possessor of untold knowledge and age-old secrets. If the Koala is abused, it is said that terrible periods of drought will follow.

Bulls and Bears

On the stock exchange different investors have different names. Some are called bulls and some . . . are called bears! A bear is an investor who thinks that share prices are going to fall and so sells in anticipation of being able to buy them back at a lower price. So, a period when share prices are falling is known as a "bear market." The term "bear" is short for "bearskin jobber" which points at these investors' tendency to "sell the bear's skin before catching the bear." No, I'm not sure I get it either!

☆ *Celebrity Bear* ☆
Yogi Bear

A popular cartoon character, Yogi lives in Jellystone Park and spends most of his waking hours trying to snaffle the goodies out of the untended picnic baskets of unsuspecting tourists while doing his utmost to avoid the attentions of Ranger Smith. Yogi Bear's tolerant sidekick is little Boo-Boo. He tries to keep his best buddy out of trouble, but usually doesn't have a hope against the allure of a delicious "pic-a -nic!"

Giggly Bear

Gamekeeper: Have you ever hunted bear?

Tourist: No, but I've gone fishing in my shorts!

The World's Fussiest Eater . . .

Has got to be the furry koala bear of eastern Australia. It feeds almost exclusively on eucalyptus leaves. It feeds regularly on only half a dozen of the 500 species and prefers certain individual trees above all others. It's even choosy when it comes to specific leaves, sometimes sifting through up to 20 pounds of leaves a day to find the $1\frac{1}{4}$ pounds that it actually eats. What a fuss-pot!

The Bear Without a Smile

On October 22, 1997, the Maryville Animal Shelter called the Appalachian Bear Center (ABC) about two orphaned cubs. The bear cubs had been picked up at Lambert Acres Golf Course. They had been sighted the day before and after careful searching, no mother could be found.

Once the proper authorization had been organized the bears were soon sent to

the ABC, where they would stay until they were old enough to be able to survive on their own in the wild.

On their arrival at the ABC, their overall condition was looked at. The two little cubs – a brother and sister – were around eight months old. The ABC tries to limit human connection with the bears they rescue, so that they can be more successfully re-introduced into the wild. But, in order to make identifying them an easier process, the bears were given names. They were named after the place they were found: "Lam" (female) and "Bert" (male). It seemed to the officers in charge that the male cub was eating just fine and doing quite well, considering the circumstances, but the female looked a little sickly. "Bert" seemed well enough to be placed straight down in the main holding pens, but "Lam" was going to need a careful eye kept on her.

Over the next 36 hours the little bear cub refused to eat and appeared to be slowly losing strength. All the people at the ABC were very worried about her and decided to call Dr. Ramsay of the University of Tennessee Veterinary School.

Lam needed to be anaesthetized so that the vet could have a proper look at her. Great care needed to be taken because she was still very small – only 11 pounds at the time and young animals like this can be easily overdosed. Not only that, but even at that weight a bear can still put up a good fight!

At first the ABC team were stumped. Lam appeared to be in good condition. But when they had a closer look at her muzzle, they found a couple of nasty puncture wounds. These seemed to be bite marks – probably from another bear or maybe even a dog. And then, when Dr. Ramsay opened the little bear's mouth, it was quickly clear just what was putting her off her dinner. Most of her front teeth were missing or falling out. This little bear couldn't smile even if it wanted to!

Fortunately for Lam she was now in just the right place to get the help she needed. She was quickly sent to the veterinary hospital for X-rays and any other treatment that might be required to get her back on the road to recovery. When they had a proper look at her mouth, they were relieved to see there was not as much damage as first expected. The wound on her muzzle had caused a nasty infection in her mouth which had made her teeth fall out. But, because she was such a young bear, most of the teeth that she had lost were her baby teeth. Luckily for Lam, she would have adult teeth just waiting to grow in and take their place. So, all she needed for the time being was some antibiotics to clear up the infection, a liquid diet to help her build her strength, and a safe place to recuperate – the ABC, of course!

Kathy Wells, one of the ABC's dedicated staff, is an infant care nurse and has a very special knack for caring for extremely small and frail bears. Within a week of being carefully looked after by Kathy, Lam was gaining strength and was soon able to be placed down in the main enclosure with her brother.

After five months of care at the bear center, Lam was ready to go. On March 19, 1998 she was captured down in the pens and given another thorough check-up. This time she passed with flying colors – a young, healthy, chubby bear. She was placed in a transport cage in care of the Tennessee Wildlife Resources Agency and released in Cherokee National Forest where she still lives to this day. And . . . she's probably smiling now too!

Did you know...?

The largest nests in the world are built by bald eagles. They can weigh up to three tons – that's as much as three small cars!

Giggly Bear

What *do* animals read in zoos?

Gnus papers!

Big Boys

Two of the heaviest ever land mammals are reported to have been bears. In 1960, a polar bear estimated to weigh 2,000 pounds was shot in the Chukchi Sea, Alaska. It was said to measure 11ft 3in from nose to tail over its body contours, 4ft 10in round the body and 1ft 5in around the paws. A kodiak bear named "Goliath" from the Space Farms Zoo, New Jersey, USA reportedly weighed more than 2,000 pounds in the early 1980s. That's a couple of very big bears.

Giggly Bear

Did you hear about the snake who had a cold?

She had to viper nose!

Top-notch Teddy

A record price was paid for a teddy bear in December 1994. A Japanese businessman, Yoshihiro Sekiguchi, paid a staggering £110,000 ($183,000) for a Steiff bear named "Teddy Girl." That was more than 18 times Christies' (the auction house's) estimated value.

Did you know...?

Polar bears taught man a thing or two. It was through watching polar bears at work that Inuit people found the best way to hunt seals: by sitting in front of a hole in the ice and waiting for the poor unsuspecting fellas to pop up for a breather! Then, wallop – seal for dinner again, dear!

Giggly Bear

Why did the two boa constrictors get married?

Because they had a crush on each other!

Ickle Babies

Giant pandas may be just that . . . giant, but their cubs weigh as little as $1/4$ pound at birth. That's about the same as an apple!

The Birth of Nanook

The Inuit people of the frozen north see bears and humans as members of the same family who simply no longer live together. Legend has it that the first bears were actually the children of an Eskimo couple who gave birth to a set of twins who were a little hairier than might have been expected! These big furry babies were called Nanook. But, shortly after they were born, their mother got a bit twitchy about their rather peculiar appearance and abandoned them to the elements on a frozen ice field. One made his way toward the icy waters and the other trotted inland to see what he could find. Later, the couple had another two sons – not nearly as furry as the first pair! After many years had passed the two boys decided they would head off hunting one morning and set off across the snow – one toward the water and one inland. The first son, alone on an ice field in the frozen sea came across a polar bear and recognized him to be none other than his long-ago abandoned elder brother. The other brother too had had such a meeting, but this time with a brown bear whom he met on the tundra, and who turned out to be the other abandoned twin. The bears told the brothers that they had forgiven their mother for what she had done, and since then an inseparable bond was formed between man and bear. The people of the far North see the bear as a friend, an ancestor and even a spiritual father.

Inuits do kill polar bears, but they would never, ever hunt more than they needed for their food and clothing. And after they have killed a polar bear, they observe a period of mourning lasting for three days for a male bear and five for a female. After all, as far as they're concerned, it could be one of their distant relatives that's just died.

Lucky Lobster

When kind-hearted Gregory Frances was 11 he saw a lobster in a supermarket tank and he just knew, when the lobster blinked at him, that it was begging to be set free. Gregory set about collecting money in a bid to set the lobster – nicknamed Lucky – free. Sadly for Gregory, and for Lucky, the lobster died before his freedom could be ensured. But . . . that didn't mean there couldn't be a happy ending. Staff at Miami's WIOD–AM radio were so impressed by Gregory's efforts, they pitched in to free another lobster on his behalf. This lobster was released off the coast of Maine where he'll hopefully live a long and happy lobster life. And the nickname of the second lobster? Luckier of course!

The story of the first ever Teddy Bear!

President Theodore Roosevelt had the nickname of Teddy. One day in 1902 he was out hunting with some friends and he wasn't doing very well – he hadn't bagged a thing all day. The people he was with then presented him with an easy target. They'd found a bear cub wandering lost in the woods and tied it to a tree ready for the president to shoot so that he wouldn't have to face the humiliation of returning from the hunting expedition empty handed. To his credit, the president refused – he'd rather face the shame than shoot a poor defenceless little animal. The kind president said, "If I kill this cub, I will never be able to look my children in the face again." Too right! And I don't think they'd have wanted to look at him either! The incident became big news in America with all the papers picking up on it. When it reached the attention of Morris and Rose Michtom, Morris, who owned a candy store, instantly had a bright idea. He quickly got Rose to put together a toy bear with little joints so that its head, arms and legs all moved, and he then placed it in the window of his store with a copy of a famous cartoon showing Roosevelt refusing to kill the bear cub and a little hand-written sign saying "Teddy's Bear." The demand became so great that soon they'd gone into mass production and, within a year, Michtom closed down his candy store and founded the Ideal Novelty and Toy Co. which is still one of the biggest toy firms in the world over ninety years later. So Teddy Bears came into existence and who would have predicted just how popular they would become. Hurrah for "Teddy" Roosevelt!

Steiff Bears

But . . . on the other side of the world, unaware of the president's historic hunting refusal, another person was thinking bears too! In late October 1902, Richard Steiff, a toy  designer who worked for his family firm in Giengen, Germany, headed off to watch a touring American circus. He was hoping it would give him some inspiration for a new range of toys. And indeed it did! When he got to the circus he saw a troupe of performing bears, standing upright in a row and it gave him an idea of the ideal animal to be turned into a cuddly toy. Bears had been made as toys before, but they hadn't been upright, they'd been down on all fours like real bears and had often been made out of real fur like real bears, too.

Richard was going to change all that, he was going to make a bear toy which stood up and had joints, like a doll, so that its arms and legs and head could all be moved. The rest of the Steiff family liked the idea and so Richard set to work drawing up his designs. Unaware of the "teddy bear" mania that had hit the States, the Steiff bear went into production in 1903, when it made its appearance at the Spring Toy Fair at Leipzig. It was, at that time, called "Friend Petz." Apparently Richard nearly went home in disappointment as nobody seemed interested in his exciting new product, but just as he was packing his things to go, an American toy buyer came up to him, grabbed the bear, and ordered 3000 of the little fellows right there on the spot. The Teddy Bear was born and on his way to international stardom.

Today, Steiff bears are still some of the most sought after by collectors and can fetch fantastic amounts at auction. So before granny gives her old ted away to charity, you'd better check the label first!

The Bear who Split a Continent

A legend of the Chukchi Peninsula in Siberia, opposite Alaska, starts in a time when Asia and America were joined together. One day, a big polar bear challenged a Chukchi hunter to a duel. He must have been incredibly brave (or incredibly stupid!) because he agreed to give it a go! The fight that followed was like one never seen before, as man and bear struggled to win out over each other. And as they stood exchanging blows on the strip of land that, at the time, separated the Pacific Ocean from the Arctic Ocean, the force of their punches was so great that the very ground beneath them began to crumble and they found themselves being pushed further and further apart. Now, if you look on a map at the Bering Strait which separates Asia from America – you'll know just how it became like that.

Kiss that Fish

When Ralph Williams of Telford in England saw his neighbor's prized carp floating on the top of his pond during a summer storm, he didn't pause for thought. He jumped straight over Terry Flockhart's fence, grabbed Brownie the fish, lifted it out of the pond and got straight to work giving it mouth-to-mouth resuscitation. Then, just to be extra sure he had done all he could, he gave it a quick heart massage before being satisfied that it was going to make it, and returning it to the water. The 16-inch long fish is not only valued for its good looks and grace but for the price-tag it commands too. People are willing to pay around £200 ($330) to be the proud owner of a Koi Carp. Caring Ralph saved Brownie's life even though he's reported to have said that the fish wasn't too tasty, "it's not like kissing a girl," he said! Well, I should think not!

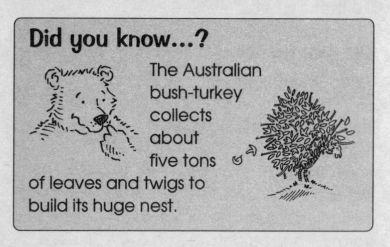

Did you know...?

The Australian bush-turkey collects about five tons of leaves and twigs to build its huge nest.

★ *Celebrity Bear* ★
Barney the Bear

A dozy cartoon critter who's always trying to get a bit of rest. He's a bear whose desire to hibernate is constantly thwarted by a pair of pesky chipmunks who love nothing better than practical jokes – especially when they're at Barney's expense!

Tiny Tortoise

Caring staff at Bristol Zoo in the UK are doing their best to ensure the survival of one of the world's most endangered species. Their attempts at breeding Egyptian tortoises paid off in July 1999 with the birth of triplets! The three tiny Tortoises Antony, Cleopatra, and Sphinx weighed in at less than half an ounce when they hatched at the zoo and even at a month old were still only 1 inch long. Ahh sweet!

Did you know...?

Rabbits have been known to reach a speed of 47 mph – that's one bionic bunny!

All in a Day's Work

One evening in July 1997 Daryl Ratajczak was getting ready to do the daily bear feeding at the Appalachian Bear Center. At that time there were three adult bears on site, two waiting for homes and one that had been injured inside Great Smoky Mountain National Park.

It was a typical summer day in East Tennessee, hot and very humid. It was about half an hour before dusk so Daryl decided to go down and get on with feeding the bears. At this point in time, the porch for the center was comprised of a large wooden door resting on cinder blocks, which Daryl and his wife had nicknamed the "dorch." As Daryl hopped off the dorch and rounded the trailer to go down to the maintenance building to get the food, he heard a tremendous crashing through the brush directly behind the building he was heading toward. This didn't worry him too much as his neighbors have a couple of large dogs which are often running around near to the ABC. Knowing what nice dogs they are and that they always kept well away from the bear pens Daryl really wasn't too concerned – he was sure it was just Clyde, a rather chubby, black Lab making his rounds.

So Daryl carried on as normal, gathering together the food he needed to feed the bears that night. It consisted mostly of fresh produce: apples, peaches, grapes, and loads of berries, as well as their daily ration of fresh acorns and hickory nuts. Daryl threw all of these delicious treats into the five gallon buckets he always uses to carry the food down to the pens and then locked up the maintenance building. As he headed off with his buckets, he decided that he'd take the longer path down to the pens so that he could say hi to his buddy Clyde when he saw him.

Daryl thought Clyde must already have become bored with waiting as, although he looked out for him, he was nowhere to be seen. What Daryl did notice though, was that it was extremely quiet. Not only was it quiet . . . it was silent – no cicadas, no birds, no frogs from the nearby pond. Nothing. But Daryl didn't have too much time to think about it – the light was fading, and he had a bunch of hungry bears to feed.

Inside the pens, all was normal except for one thing. Normally, the bears

 would be resting or playing like bears like to play – knocking down small trees for no apparent reason and rough-housing with each other. But this time something was up. Two of the bears were pacing back and forth, almost as if they were agitated or scared. Daryl really didn't know what to make of it, but wasn't quite sure what he could do about it either, so he simply finished feeding them and locked up their pens safely for the night.

As he was leaving to go back up to the trailer he paused at the corner of the bear pens and tried to figure out what was bothering them. There was still dead silence in the forest and the last of the daylight was fading fast. As he stood at the corner of the pens straining his eyes to gaze down into the valley below . . .  he heard a sound that made his heart do a somersault in his chest. It was a "huff." The sort of huff people make when they take a deep breath and then let it all out at once. Daryl had heard this sort of huff hundreds of times before. It was just the sort of huff a bear makes when it's really irritated or annoyed about something. He knew from his own experiences at the ABC that this was the sort of huff his bears would use to say, "I'm really fed up right now, so you better keep out of my way . . . if you know what's good for you that is!" But Daryl's bears were safely penned up on his right and . . . the sound was coming from his left!

Needless to say Daryl didn't feel too comfortable. He was standing out in the open with some delicious-smelling buckets in his hands, dripping with berry juice, with a rather aggravated bear standing not too far away! It was definitely time to head back to the trailer!

It didn't take too long to walk back up the trail and put the buckets back inside the maintenance building. In total it probably only took about two or three seconds Daryl was moving so fast. And, having dropped the buckets off, he began to feel a bit better and decided to sit by the campfire in the hope of catching a glimpse of his huffy visitor. But as he sat in the twilight he soon changed his mind as his wife called from the "dorch" to say that their neighbor had called to say "watch out" as the biggest bear she'd ever seen had just been trying to get up on her porch. Apparently, good old Clyde had scared the bear away. But the neighbor said that even that was a miracle as the bear was at least three times bigger than the faithful dog. That would put the bear in the 300–400 pound range, a "monster" for this part of Tennessee. And Daryl had to admit to himself – a job at the ABC is nothing if not exciting!

Did you know...?

 That the energy produced by the heat of a cow's belches in just one day would be enough to generate central heating in the average sized house for up to a week! That's some hot breath!

Lucky bear

As long ago as 1066 BC in China, pandas were owned by very important people. They were believed to have mystical powers and were thought to act like lucky charms, warding off evil spirits, disease and disaster. I'm not sure quite how lucky it was for the Panda, though!

Did you know...?

A Prairie Dog isn't a dog at all but a large rodent. Hmmm – a rat the size of a dog – now that's scary!

Dog's Eye View

During the 1999 total solar eclipse that was visible on August 11 over most of Europe and much of Asia, people were warned not to look directly at the sun for fear of damaging their eyes. But some people thought not only of themselves but of their animals too and dog-lover Amanda Desantis even came up with a range of shades just perfect for pups, which she called her "pucci" range!

Trial by . . . bears!

There was once one bear who got in trouble with the law. In 1499 a brown bear was put on trial in Germany. He'd been frightening the life out of local peasants and they'd had enough. Unfortunately for them, but luckily for the bear, the law stated that the bear had the right to be tried by a jury made up of his peers (that meant twelve other brown bears!). It seemed no one was that keen to rustle up the jury, so the bear was released with a bit of a ticking off – sounds bear-enough to me!

Did you know...?

 That six large fire-flies could provide enough light for you to read this book by – forget taking a torch to bed, go for bug-power instead!

How the Panda Became Black-and-White

According to Chinese legend, the panda was not always black-and-white, but used to be just white (a bit of competition for the polar bear there!). It's because of a very sad event that the pandas got their wonderfully distinctive markings. It was all

because of a family of pandas who were attending the burial of a little girl. They were very sad and, according to their tradition, had covered their hands with ash. As they cried they rubbed their eyes to wipe away their tears and lo-and-behold they left behind black rings from their ashy hands. The more sad they became the more they huddled together for comfort, giving each other a supportive hug every now and again. Of course, in doing so, they left a trail of black ash up each other's arms and legs too! And because they're such lovely, caring creatures they've kept their beautiful markings to show that they'll never forget the little girl they wept for long ago.

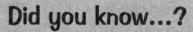

Did you know...?

An elephant's trunk can carry two gallons of water – now that's what I call a power shower!

When Is a Bear Not a Bear?

When it's a bear cat! The Civet family is a group of flesh-eating mammals closely related to cats, but with longer bodies, more pointed faces and shorter legs. The bear cat is a civet. It has long, blackish fur and is fairly common throughout the East Indies, Malaysia, Assam, and Thailand. They have long tufts of hair on their ears and they can support their whole weight from the branches of trees by their tails. Shy creatures that they are, they hide during the day and climb at night in search of food; unluckily for any creature that might find itself on that evening's menu!

Criminal Koalas

Koalas have fingerprints that are so similar to humans that quite often, when the Australian police dust for burglar fingerprints, they come up with a set of dabs belonging to one of our furry friends. As their natural habitats are encroached on, some koalas now live in quite urban locations which, on occasions, might even have been the scene of a crime! Their patterned paws aren't made that way for criminal purposes though, they just happen to be the perfect design for helping the little fellows out when they want to climb up their favorite eucalyptus trees for a snack and a nap.

Did you know...?

A female starfish produces two million eggs a year. Unfortunately for her, she has to, as 99 percent of them are eaten by other fish. Oh boo-hoo!

Foiled Royal

King James I of England (VI of Scotland) was obsessed with lions – the symbol on his Scottish crown. He bred them and kept them in the moat of the Tower of London where they could roam in restricted freedom. James lived in a time when people didn't care very much about animals and often used them for "entertainment" even if it involved terrible cruelty to the animals concerned. A popular sport of the time was known as bear-baiting. During this awful event a bear would be chained to a post and then attacked by dogs. It was a fight to the death and people bet on the results. Apparently though, even this wasn't exciting enough for James and he decided that it would be much more fun to have the bear attacked by a lion – nice guy! But, unfortunately for him, he didn't bank on the animals being smarter than he was. He put the two hapless creatures in a ring together where they simply sat and stared at each other and refused to fight. Hard luck James – round one to the lion *and* the bear I think!

Did you know...?

The owl is the only creature able to turn its head in a complete circle – so remember, no talking behind an owl's back, sides or front!

Poetic Justice

When the poet Byron discovered that he would not be allowed to keep a dog in his room he decided to get his own back and kept a pet bear instead – after all, it didn't say anything in the rules about that!

Did you know...?

Earthworms over seven feet long are to be found in some parts of Western Australia. Still, they're very good for the garden you know!

Scent Wild

Experts trying to encourage some rather shy ocelots to breed at Dallas Zoo in Texas, thought they'd encourage them through their sense of smell. They thought that rat droppings would be just the thing to get the ocelots going, but were surprised to find that the smell the ocelots liked best was . . . Calvin Klein's Obsession for Men! Those little critters sure do have expensive tastes!

Did you know...?

The Canje Pheasant, a native of Guyana, isn't a pheasant at all – it isn't even a bird! It's a kind of flying skunk which gives off an overwhelmingly unpleasant odor, if frightened, as it sails over people's heads.

An Unforgettable Christmas

The fall and winter season of 1997 brought some unexpected challenges to the Appalachian Bear Center. Besides the extraordinary amount of cubs that came in, they were faced with a number of unique and very high-stress situations! Thankfully, with the dedicated help of a few volunteers they were able to make it through a Christmas none of them will ever be able to forget.

As Curator of the ABC, Daryl Ratajczak didn't think it was fair to ask any of his team of volunteers to spoil their vacation by having to "bear sit" on Christmas Day. So, he and his wife Sandy decided to spend their first Christmas together alone in the trailer at the bear center. Though "alone" isn't quite

the case as there was actually a party of sixteen to cater for! – Daryl, Sandy, Smoky (their dog) and thirteen mischievous roly poly little black bear cubs!

Daryl and Sandy were going to be looking after all of them

67

on Christmas Day, and then would head off for their break on December 26. But soon . . . even those plans were in jeopardy.

Christmas Day started out well. Santa had been good to the couple and they were beginning to get excited about their long trip back to Buffalo, N.Y. where they were going to spend some time with close family and friends. Daryl had the "bear sitters" all lined up for the next week and he and Sandy were packed and ready to go. It only needed one last check on the bear pens and their cargo of cubs at the end of the day, and then they'd be ready to be off.

When Daryl went on his rounds, everything looked fine. All thirteen tiny fur balls were nestled in the trees dreamily sleeping away winter. And then . . . something terrible happened . . . and Daryl could hardly believe his eyes. As he made his way around the northeast corner of the pen he paused to look at the last group of cubs comfortably resting in a large crooked pine. "Rocky," "Calderwood" and "Houdini" were happily snoozing the winter away, when suddenly their world literally came down around them. The tree they were sleeping in snapped at the base and began to fall. Daryl watched as all three scared and confused cubs hung on for dear life. What made everything even worse was that the path the tree was taking was going to drop the bears right on top of the electric fence!

It was at this point that luck (or fate) intervened. The tiniest of branches from a nearby tree happened to catch the falling pine with its precious cargo. With a sudden jerk the tree became caught on the other tree's branches and hung precariously

 dangling in mid air with the three little cubs trying to cling on for all they were worth. In fact, "Houdini" was jerked so violently, she lost grip with her back legs and was left dangling by her front paws only just above the electric fence. Daryl watched, his heart thumping in his chest as the little bear had the good sense to pull herself back up and reverse up the tree to a more secure position.

The cubs seemed to be fine, but they were still left in a tree that was only a hair's breadth away from coming down altogether. Two of the cubs seemed to cotton on quickly to their predicament and started heading down the tree right away. Both Rocky and Calderwood paused after each step. The bounce from each of their movements pushed the pine a few inches closer to disaster. And when Rocky and Calderwood finally made it to the ground, and to safety, only little Houdini was left in desperate straits.

Although this whole event only took a few seconds, Daryl found himself standing with his mouth hanging open, staring in disbelief.

He waited for everything to settle down and then walked to a better vantage point so that he could check the exact seriousness of Houdini's situation. It wasn't good. The branch that was holding the huge pine up was only a few inches in diameter and bending in a very worrying way. What made things worse was that the cub had worked out how much danger she was in and had tried to crawl into an adjacent tree. With every shift in her weight the tree slipped a few inches and the base of the pine moaned under the stress that was on it. This scared the cub and she settled in, determined not to move.

Finally, Daryl's heart began to beat again as he tried to work out just what he should do. He made a mad dash up to the trailer to find Sandy putting the last of their bags into the car. He explained the situation and then got straight on the phone. Thankfully not everyone was away on vacation and he soon managed to get hold of Tom Faulkner, an ABC board member. Daryl told Tom what was up and Tom got busy phoning around and, amazingly, managed to round up a crew from Ogle's Tree Cutting Service.

By the time everyone arrived at the center it was well after dark. Everyone got

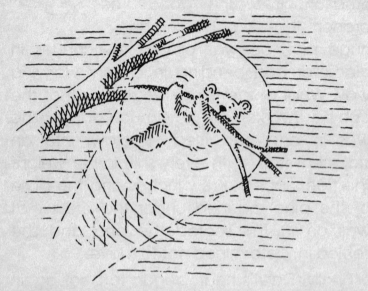

flashlights and headed down to the pens hoping the conifer and cub remained intact. Luckily, the large pine was still hung up in the other tree but "Houdini" was still nestled in its branches. This meant there was no way the crew would be able to remove the tree that night.

With flashlights in hand and ropes in tow, the tree cutters did their work and made sure that the tree was secure for the night.

Being in the pens at night with six other cubs meant Tom and Daryl had to keep a close watch over where the other bears were. Thankfully, due to the "hands off" approach at ABC, all the bears remained nervous of humans and kept their distance. When all was secure the Ogle's staff were sent home for the night to get some rest, before having to return in the morning to remove the tree.

And, by the time morning came, little Houdini had worked out what was best for her – she'd finally managed to make her way safe and sound down to solid ground.

And yes, Sandy and Daryl did make it home for the vacations after all!

Lucky Lottie the Lobster

Fishermen trawling off the Channel Islands between the UK and France were surprised at just what they pulled up in their net – a pink lobster!

Although, once cooked, many lobsters become orange in color, in nature they range from a muddy red through brown and black to dark blue. The reason for their rather dull natural coloring is a matter of survival. In order to avoid becoming the tasty dinner of any

number of deep-sea predators it's best if the lobsters can camouflage themselves and avoid being seen altogether.

When the fishermen that found Lottie clapped eyes on her, they knew she was quite a special crustacean, but they didn't realize quite how special until they took her to marine experts to have her checked out. The fishy fiends checked Lottie over and declare that judging by her size and weight she was at least 15 years old – pretty good going for a lobster at the best of times, but for one that stood out from the crowd like Lottie, it was really quite amazing!

But for once, Lottie's coloring was in her favor, as no one wanted her to live out the rest of her days in constant danger on the sea bed; she was given a safe new

Did you know...?

Apes, guinea pigs, and human beings are the only mammals capable of producing vitamin C in their own bodies . . .

home at Bournemouth's Oceanarium where she'll soon be one of the main attractions. The likelihood of a lobster being born without any dark pigment in its shell is about one in 200,000, but the chances of it then reaching adulthood are about one in a million! Lucky Lottie made it through, against all odds, and now looks set to have an even longer and less stressful life at the bottom of her very own tank!

Bern's Bears

The Swiss city of Bern is famous for its love of bears. And in 1832 a statue of the bear-goddess Artio was dug up in the city. She was worshiped by the Helvetii, a Celtic people who inhabited the western part of Switzerland over 2,000 years ago. The city, founded in 1191, was named after its bears. One appears on the earliest known town seal, made in 1224.

Did you know...?

That a snake at London Zoo was fitted with a glass eye!

The Dance of the Grizzly Bear

Grizzly Bear is one of the animal people, or spirits, in Native North American mythology. He was worshiped for his curative powers by Fox and California tribes. They had a ceremonial Grizzly Bear Dance which included a tribesman in bearskins and a mask impersonating the great bear. Since the Kootenais believed that Grizzly Bear was in charge of all plants, roots, and berries, their dance was performed at the beginning of the berry-picking season. It was a prayer to the bear, asking that he tell them where to find the berries.

Did you know...?

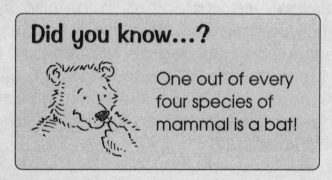

One out of every four species of mammal is a bat!

Bear-ly Alive. Thank Heavens!

Three tiny black bear cubs which were "bear"ly alive when they were orphaned this past winter have a much brighter future thanks to the Appalachian Bear Center (ABC).

In late January, a logging company in Newbern, North Carolina cut down a large tree which was to be harvested for its lumber. Unfortunately, the tree was home to four bears, a large female and three newborn cubs. Although the incident was not fatal to any of the bears, it was enough to scare off the mother, leaving behind three tiny orphans which were only a few days old.

Weighing around a pound each, the cubs were rescued by Lynn Uwell Combs, wife of Steven Combs who worked for the logging company. She in turn placed a call to the Appalachian Bear Center seeking advice on how to care for the extremely young bears. Knowing all too well the urgency of the situation, Daryl Ratajczak, Curator of the ABC, talked Lynn through the basic immediate care the cubs would need and put the wheels into motion for the cubs' eventual transfer to East Tennessee.

After all the formalities were ironed out, the three babies were delivered to the center by the North Carolina Wildlife Resources Commission on Friday, January 29.

The cubs, which were soon nicknamed Newbern, Caro, and Lina (after their birthplace), were in stable condition; however, their future remained uncertain.

Typically the ABC adheres to a strict "hands off" policy when rehabilitating black bears. But, these cubs were still babies and couldn't eat solid foods yet, so that would mean they needed to be bottle fed every four hours. So, human contact was inevitable.

So, a special plan was devised. The plan called for the cooperation of a number of state and federal agencies. Therefore, the ABC contacted the North Carolina Wildlife Resources Commission, the Tennessee Wildlife Resource Agency, the University of Tennessee and the National Park Service and received permission to carry out a detailed "adoption" procedure. This procedure called for the ABC to care for the babies until wild surrogate mothers were found, who, it was hoped, would then "adopt" the orphans. The other agencies were in charge of finding the suitable mothers.

In the meantime, the ABC had its hands full trying to care for the baby cubs. To make their stay at the Bear Center as untraumatic as possible, the staff had to

create a friendly atmosphere for the young bears. Their temporary den was a large storage container which was kept in the back room of the trailer. It was lined with a number of clean towels and had a large "Momma Bear" (cuddly toy) placed inside for comfort. There was also a ticking clock wrapped in a washcloth near the cubs to simulate a mother's heartbeat. Warm water bottles were then wrapped in towels and placed in the pen every four hours to provide warmth. A heating pad placed under one end of the box also provided an additional source of heat. If any of the cubs became too hot, it simply crawled a few inches away to a cooler area.

Newbern, a male, along with Caro and Lina, two females, were then fed a special formula every 3–4 hours around the clock! Considering it took almost an hour for preparation, feeding, and clean-up, there was not much time to do anything else. So it's very lucky for the little bears that the ABC has such a dedicated staff of volunteers who willingly helped out to make this task a little easier. So I think it's safe to say that, although they'd lost their mother, these particular cubs were very well cared for little bears.

Although Newbern, Caro, and Lina, adjusted quite well to their new home at the Center, the ABC knew it was in the best interest of the cubs to find foster homes in the wild as soon as they possibly could. Any prolonged contact with people would only end up harming their chances of once again roaming free in the wild.

Therefore, in February, each orphan was introduced into the litter of separate female bears within the National Park system. Since the new mothers were in the middle of their hibernation, they weren't fully aware of what was going on inside their dens (they were sedated for safety purposes as well). By the time they were fully awake in the spring, they wouldn't even realize they had an "extra" cub in their litter. Luckily, this method of adoption has proven to be quite successful; it seems momma bears have more than enough love to go around.

The first cub fostered to a wild mother was Lina. She ended up going to an 11-year-old female inside the Big South Fork River and Recreational Area. Lina's new "mom" was slightly over 200 pounds, and had three cubs of her own. Her den was located underneath the rootball of a large blown down tree and was nearly inaccessible due to the tremendous amount of ground cover surrounding it. Finally, Newbern and Caro went to surrogate mothers inside the Great Smoky Mountains National Park on the last weekend in February. Both females were in excellent condition and each had three cubs of her own.

Although the fate of the cubs will not be known until next year, everyone wishes them luck and feels much better knowing they have the best possible mothers to look after them – real bear mothers of course!

Did you know...?

 The Mountain Devil, a lizard-like creature which lives in Australia, never drinks. It absorbs tiny drops of dew through its skin.

Judge the Bear

Baylor University in Waco, Texas had a rather unusual mascot – a North American black bear called Judge. The first bear became mascot in the late 1920s having been abandoned in the town by a traveling circus. A caring student suggested to the president of Baylor that the bear could have a new role as the school's official mascot. The student then said that he would be more than happy to care for the bear if, in return, the university would give him – the student – free tuition. Hmmm – smarter than the average bear I'd say!

All Seeing Phil

Punxsutawney Phil, known as the "seer of seers" is the resident groundhog at Gobbler's Knob in Punxsutawney, Pennsylvania. He's a very special fella as it's

up to him to predict the late, or early, coming of spring! The Punxsutawney Groundhog Club, founded in 1887, meets up every year on Groundhog Day, February 2, to observe Phil's amazing weather prediction.

If he comes out of his burrow, sees his shadow, and goes back in, there will be six more weeks of winter. The tradition came to America with German immigrants. Back in their homeland, they had watched the reaction of badgers to work out whether or not spring was on its way. But finding a distinct lack of the black-and-white creatures in sunny Pennsylvania, they had to make do with the next best thing – and groundhogs seemed to fit the bill perfectly! Apparently groundhogs really are just as good as their badger chums at predicting the seasonal forecast. The Punxsutawney Groundhog Club claims that in all its years – that's right from 1887 – good old Phil has never been wrong once!

And, amazingly enough, Phil is not alone. In Sun Prairie, Wisconsin, there's another groundhog with the same job. At 7 a.m. on February 2 he's doing just the same as Phil. It's an exciting occasion where reporters throng and adults drink Jimmy's health with a drink called Moose Milk. In twenty-three years of predicting the coming of spring, five Jimmies have had a go, and out of those twenty-three years they've between them been right eighteen times – not quite as good as Phil, but not bad, not bad at all!

Giggly Bear

Two elephants wanted to go swimming.

They couldn't – they only had one pair of trunks!

The Bear with the Golden Butt!

A folk story from India tells the tale of a poor farmer who had been working away from home for many months. In that time he had been saving his money to take back to his home village. He had worked hard and saved a lot of cash and had wrapped it up in his dhoti (a long cloth wrapped around his waist) to carry home to his family.

On the way home, though, he grew tired. It was a scorching hot day and the farmer decided to take a few minutes rest under the shade of a nearby fig tree. He sat down, leaned back against the tree, and was so weary that he was soon fast asleep.

He was woken, a while later, by a strange growling sound. As he struggled back to wakefulness the sound grew louder and the farmer heard the cracking of the branches above him as something began to climb down the tree toward him. As he stared up, a large, brown bear emerged – heading straight for him!

The farmer didn't know what to do; he was frozen to the spot, afraid to run away in case the bear gave chase, but afraid to stay where he was in case he ended up as a bear's dinner. Finally he pulled himself to his feet, his back still against the tree and waited for the bear to finish its descent.

The bear, meanwhile, slowly shuffled its way down the tree. It was hugging the trunk with both arms as it shimmied down toward the farmer. And as it reached the bottom, the farmer quickly ran round to

the other
side of the tree
and grabbed the
bear by the paws.
They stood facing
each other,
with the tree
between
them. The bear
began circling the
tree and, as the
farmer had tight hold of its paws, he had no
choice but to do the same. As they moved
slowly around the tree the coins that had
been so carefully tucked into the farmer's
dhoti, began dropping to the ground, one
at a time. The farmer really was in a fix!

Just then, a rich (and rather greedy) money-
lender was passing by. As soon as he heard
the tinkling of coins he stopped in his tracks.
He followed the sound of the money all the
way to the fig tree. What he saw there almost
defied belief. There was a man and bear, paw
in hand, gracefully dancing around a fig tree,

one step at a time. The money-lender could hardly believe his eyes. But his disbelief got even greater when he saw what lay on the ground at their feet – a trail of gold coins!

The money-lender looked at the coins with greed in his eyes and went to talk to the farmer to ask him just what was going on. At that point the farmer had a flash of inspiration – and he told the money-lender a bit of a tale. "This bear is magical," he said.

"How do you mean?" asked the money-lender.

"Well," the farmer replied, "the coins you see on the ground come from the bear. Each time we go around the tree money drops out of his rear end! It's really quite simple."

The money-lender was amazed but also rather jealous. He would rather like to get his hands on this bear's fortune. Thinking he was being rather clever he tapped the farmer on the shoulder and said, "You look rather tired my friend, if you like I'll take over and you can take a rest."

The farmer nodded quietly as the money-lender eagerly took his place putting both his hands over the bear's paws as the farmer stepped out of the way.

With relief, the farmer gathered his money off the ground, tucked it carefully back into his dhoti and tied it tightly. And as he set off for home, the last view he had over his shoulder was of a big brown bear and a greedy money-lender dancing happily around and around a tree!

Did you know...?

That all animals with backbones, including humans, are descended from fish!

Pretty Perfect for Polly

A couple who are bird-bonkers have bequeathed £100,000 ($165,000) to their 60 pet parrots. They can't bear to think of their beloved birds receiving anything but the best treatment, even after they're no longer around to give it, so they're leaving the money to ensure that all their birds can have a happy life at a top-notch sanctuary after they've gone.

Paul and Christine Forman, decided the parrots will need the money more than their relatives will, as they can live to be 80 years old and cost a fortune to feed. And Christine even admits that if it came to a choice between humans and parrots – she'd pick her feathered friends every time!

Giggly Bear

What do you get if you cross a blackbird with a coconut?

A raven nut-case!

The Bear Man

The Native Americans have lots of stories about animals and that includes bears. They have great respect as a people for all things on Mother Earth. All living things are considered sacred because they were created by the Great Spirit.

One story that comes from the Pawnee nation (who eventually settled in what is now called Oklahoma) is about a boy who was very much like a bear . . .

Before the boy was born, his father had

gone hunting near to their camp. During this time he had come across a wounded bear cub. He was a kind-hearted man and looking at the little bundle of fur he felt unable to just walk away and let it die, helplessly. So he paused, bent down and tied some Indian tobacco around the little bear's neck saying, "The Great Spirit, Tirawa, will take care of you. This tobacco charm will help you. I hope, in turn, that your fellow bears will one day take care of my son when he is born, and help him grow into a great and wise man."

When he returned to his camp he told his wife about the bear he had met and what had passed between them. There is a Pawnee superstition which says that if people look into the eyes of an animal before their own child is born, that child will inherit the ways of that animal. The father-to-be had to confess that as he had talked to the little bear cub, he had looked directly into its dark brown eyes.

And so it was, that when the boy was born he did indeed seem to have habits like those of a bear and the older he got the more like a bear he became. And he often went off into the forest by himself to pray to the Great Bear Spirit.

Eventually the boy reached manhood and one of his tasks was to lead a Pawnee war party out against their enemies the Sioux. Unfortunately for the Pawnee braves an ambush lay in wait and they were sitting ducks. Every single man on the mission was killed including the bear man.

In that region, there were always many bears and so, of course, it was only a matter of time before some bears came upon the dead bodies of the warring party. The bear-man had suffered terribly and his body had been scattered across the plain. Despite this, a she-bear recognized him at once as the man who had spent his time praying to the Great Bear Spirit and sacrificing tobacco to them, as well as making up songs about them and doing his best to make sure they were protected.

She spent some time gathering together the remains of the bear-man and placing them all together in the right order. This done she lay down upon his body and worked her medicine on him until he showed signs of life. Slowly he regained his strength and when he was strong enough to be moved the she-bear led him carefully to her den.

He then spent some time with the bears, recovering his health and learning from them. They taught him all the things they knew – which was much, for the bears are the wisest of animals. They had both strength and wisdom and they told the bear-man that he should not forget them and that he should keep his bear ways, for that is what would finally make him a success as a wise and powerful leader.

Finally the she-bear told him, "The cedar tree shall be your protector. It never grows old, is ever fresh and green, it is Tirawa's gift. If a thunderstorm comes while you are at home with your family, throw some cedar wood upon the fire and you will all be safe."

When the bear-man eventually arrived back at his camp, his people were amazed to see him. They felt sure that all their braves had been killed. The bear-man explained how it was that the bears had saved him and that without them he would have remained dead for ever. The next day he took gifts of tobacco, beads, buffalo meat, and sweet-smelling clay back to his bear family. The she-bear embraced him and said, "As my fur has touched you, you will be great. As my hands have touched you, you will be fearless. As my mouth touches your mouth, you will be wise."

They parted on this bond. And, as time passed, the bear-man did become great and wise and was the best warrior of his tribe. It was he that started the Pawnee Bear Dance which is still danced today.

Paws for thought . . .

The widow of a wealthy Australian fur dealer left a million dollars to a pair of polar bears in Perth zoo. Guess they reminded her of a favorite coat she once had!

Seal of Approval

It was a doubly happy day when Titch the gray harbor seal gave birth at Natureland seal sanctuary in Skegness, Britain, because it wasn't just one little pup she produced – but two! A pair of adorable twins arrived in August 1999 and that's extremely rare. In fact, they're only the second set of twin seal pups to be reared in captivity anywhere in the world.

At first they'll feed on their mother's milk before moving on to solids (fish!), after about three weeks before they're eventually big and strong enough to be released into the wild. But before that can happen, sanctuary staff have to be happy that the twins know how to fend for themselves, catching fish and keeping out of harm's way. Before they leave they'll be tagged so that the caring Natureland staff can keep an eye on them even when they're out in the wild.

Nine years ago Natureland became the first place in the world to successfully rear twin seals when a seal called Franny gave birth to twins and it looks like they're well on the way to repeating the success with little Salt and Pepper.

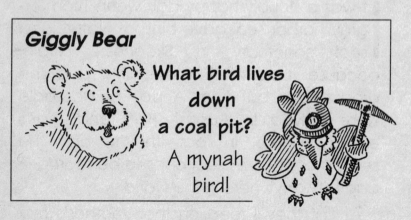

Giggly Bear

What bird lives down a coal pit?

A mynah bird!

Cheeky Chipmunk

According to the Native American Seneca Indians the grizzly bear is responsible for the stripes on a chipmunk's back. Apparently a chipmunk didn't have stripes originally, he used to be plain brown. But one day he met a bear who said he was strong enough to stop the sun coming up. The chipmunk teased the bear, telling him to prove it. The bear tried and, of course, failed. This made the bear very cross and made the little chipmunk laugh which, of course, made the bear even crosser. At this point the chipmunk thought it might be a good idea to get out of the bear's way so he made a run for it. But, just as he got to his hole, the bear caught up. The bear made a grab for the little chipmunk and just caught his back with his long claws. As the chipmunk wriggled away, three long scratches were left down each side of his back and those are the dark stripes that the chipmunk bears even to this day.

Paws for thought . . .

Hercules the grizzly bear was voted "Scottish Showbusiness Personality of the Year" for 1981 – beating such impressive competition as Sean Connery and Billy Connolly!

Libearty for Bears

In 1992 the World Society for the Protection of Animals (WSPA) launched its Libearty campaign, the first and only campaign aimed specifically at bears, working to eradicate cruelty toward them in captivity and fight their slide toward extinction in the wild. The campaign was desperately needed – five out of eight species of bears were in danger of extinction and all bears are under threat.

Initially the main focuses of their campaign were the terrible abuses suffered by bears in the name of entertainment in countries such as Greece, Turkey and Pakistan. Turkey and Greece had a long history of dancing bears, used to entertain tourists, but at great cost to the bears themselves. In Turkey dancing bears were actually illegal, but the laws were rarely enforced – the government claimed that it would be pointless capturing all the illegally held dancing bears, as they then would have nowhere to put them and no one available who was properly trained in their care. Libearty set about putting this right, building sanctuaries to house the bears which contained vet's centers for their medical needs and large semi-wild enclosures to give them a pleasant and safe place to live.

For the first such sanctuary they needed to raise $150,000. They launched their campaign in the UK and got such a fantastic response from a public outraged by the dreadful treatment these noble creatures had suffered that they raised the money in three short months and were able to build their first shelter in Greece.

Working closely with the police to confiscate the bears, they then can come under the expert care of Libearty's teams of dedicated vets and support staff. The bears will be freed from the chains that have held them for years and the ring they have had to wear through their sensitive snout will be carefully removed, as will their horribly heavy collar.

Libearty now has a sanctuary in Turkey, too, and feels confident that they have been key in wiping out this cruel form of "entertainment" hopefully, permanently. Bears that have been taken as cubs and trained up in this unnatural behavior and are always in close proximity to humans would find it very difficult to adjust back to life in the wild. They need to be in a secure place that allows them freedom of movement, but where their needs are met, and where they can be constantly supervised and looked after. Libearty campaigns tirelessly not just for the rescuing and rehabilitation of those bears suffering needlessly at the hands of man, but also for the foresight to look after the bears' natural habitats and to stop the poaching of bears for their skins, paws and gall bladders – which are considered to be of great medicinal value in many parts of Asia.

Giggly Bear

What *do* Polar Bears have for lunch?

Ice burgers!

★ *Celebrity Bear* ★

Paddington Bear

Named after the London train station where he was found by the Brown family, Paddington Bear is a popular British children's books character. The little bear was sent all the way from Peru to England by his aunt and was found with a small tag around his neck which read "please look after this bear" which, fortunately for Paddington, the Brown family were only too pleased to do – it's just a shame their neighbor, Mr. Gruber, wasn't quite so keen on the furry fellow! Easily recognizable in his floppy hat, Wellington boots and duffle coat, Paddington has won the hearts of generations of children and adults alike.

Paws for thought

At Wildlife Images Animal Refuge in Oregon, a grizzly bear called Griz and a little cat are the best of friends. It all started when the cat was a tiny kitten and unwittingly wandered into the big bears enclosure and started sniffing at his food! The staff watched amazed as the bear took a bit of food from his own plate and offered it to the kitten. Since then, the pair have become inseparable and the cat even lets the bear pick it up in its mouth and carry her around.

Retired Film Stars - A Libearty Success Story

When some of Hungary's popular actors retired, they didn't have any luxury homes with swimming pools to go to. They didn't even have a nice pad with a garden. They had nothing but tiny cages, little food and water, and the love of one man to keep them going. These stars that no one wanted any more were bears, and the man who tried to look after them was their old trainer Jozsef Kosa.

When Hungary's wildlife film industry got bored with bears they gave Jozsef and his charges the sack. With little money coming in

Jozsef was unable to keep the bears in the manner they deserved. They lived in squalid conditions, cramped in to small cages left on some wasteground near the town of Godollo, not far from Budapest. The bears were muddy and bored with no space to move and little to keep them entertained they languished in these conditions for several years before their plight came to the attention of WSPA.

But since their re-discovery, things are looking up. Peter Henderson, WSPA Project Manager has now built a specially designed 10 acre bear refuge which will be their new home. The sanctuary, near the local village of Vereseghaz was officially opened in October 1998. It is Hungary's first ever bear sanctuary and will house the forgotten film stars who range from just three years old to the ripe old age of twenty!

It's a whole new life for the bears whose new home provides them with ample wilderness to wander in as well as two natural swimming pools which they love to splash and play in. They have had specially designed artificial dens built for them, which feel just like home, and which are big enough for a few of the bears to snuggle up in together. They also have a properly equipped veterinary facility at the ready for any bear that might happen to have a sore head!

Despite the sadness of the years that had gone before, the bears all passed their medical checks without signs of injury or ill-health. It seems despite his difficult situation Mr. Kosa had tried to do his best by his bears. Sadly though, the bears can never be returned to the wild, as they have spent too long in captivity and would no longer know how to fend for themselves. But instead, they have the next best thing, a safe, secure home with room to roam free and the supervision of people who love them.

They may not be stars of the silver screen anymore, but to anyone who's seen them, they'll always be stars in their own right anyway.

If you would like further information or to make a donation to Libearty or WSPA or, if you would like to sponsor your very own bear cub, you can contact them at the following addresses:

For the United Kingdom:

WSPA UK, 2 Langley Lane, London, SW8 1TJ, United Kingdom
Phone – 0171 793 0540 Fax 0171 793 0208
Email – wspa@wspa.org.uk
Website – www.wspa.org.uk

For the USA:

WSPA USA, 29 Perkins Street, P.O. Box 190, Boston, MA 02130
Phone – + 1 617 522 7000
Email – wspa@wspausa.com

For Canada – see page 118.

For Australia

WSPA Australia, 46 Nicholson Street, St. Leonards, NSW 2065
Phone – +61 2 9901 5205
Email – kmjones@ozemail.com.au

Giggly Bear

How do you stop a herd of elephants from charging?

Take away their credit cards!

Smarter than the Average Bear . . .

An American tourist on vacation in Russia decided that he'd like to spend part of his vacation hunting for wild bears – nice guy – not! He tried to organize this event through a local Russian tourist official. The official agreed that he could set the hunt up, but decided to set the tourist up at the same time. He went off to a run-down circus and

bought a bear from them. He thought the bear would be easy pickings, the tourist would be delighted at the ease and success of his hunt, and he could make some more money  out of the whole charade. He set the tourist on his way, then dropped the bear off nearby, knowing that the hunter would soon come across it. What he hadn't counted on though, was the local postman riding by. He got such a shock at spotting a bear on his normally peaceful route that he fell off his bike. The tourist moved in for the kill, the bear, remembering his days in the circus, grabbed the bike, got on the saddle, and raced off into the sunset. Good for him!

Did you know...?

Polar bears are left-handed . . . or should that be left-pawed?!

Rocky – the Cuddly Koala

Lynne Hamilton, the Education Officer of Lone Pine Koala Sanctuary in Australia sent me this lovely story about Rocky, a rather chubby fellow, who loved a cuddle – no matter what the circumstances!

Lone Pine Koala Sanctuary is set in a beautiful rainforest setting, right on the Brisbane River just 15 minutes from the city by car. They are open to visitors daily from 7.30 a.m. to 5.00 p.m. and are the perfect place to see and learn about Australia's cutest inhabitants!

There used to be a koala called "Rocky" at the sanctuary who had to be one of the most affectionate koalas that has ever lived there. Every day the staff at the sanctuary perform three koala talks to the public. Rocky always made a point of making a grand entrance in the middle of the talk by climbing down the koala pole and up the steps to the stage where the koala talk was presented. It was almost like he heard Lynne's voice over the pa system and thought "Hm, must be time for my daily hug."

Once he reached the stage he would sit at Lynne's feet and start climbing up her legs for a big cuddle. The tourists listening to the talk would see Rocky at Lynne's feet and think he was just adorable and very affectionate as he always wanted to be

picked up and cuddled. The trouble was after holding him for about 5 to 10 minutes and trying to carry on presenting the koala talk Lynne would become completely exhausted and rather out of breath because Rocky weighed close to 22 pounds! By the time Lynne got half way through her talk she would have to make her excuses and explain to everyone how heavy he was and how difficult it was to continue talking and holding him at the same time!

But, at the end of the day, Rocky always made the koala talks at the Lone Pine Sanctuary just that little bit special for all who came to listen to them. It was very sad the day that he passed away from old age at the tender age of 8 years. Everyone was very upset for weeks afterwards. To this day there is still a beautiful picture of Rocky in the staff room at the sanctuary because he is one of those koalas that no one there will ever be able to forget – he just gave such a lot of love!

For more information on the Lone Pine Sanctuary you can contact them at:

Lone Pine Koala Sanctuary

Jesmond Road

Fig Tree Pocket

4069 Brisbane

Australia

Email: koala@koala.net

Website : www.koala.net

★ *Celebrity Bear* ★
Winnie-the-Pooh

Created by the writer A. A. Milne, Winnie-the-Pooh is a true mega-star among bears. Living in the hundred acre woods with his good friends Piglet, Eeyore and Tigger he may be a bear of very little brain, but he's got a huge heart and a very huggable honey-filled tummy.

The Withy Bears Hotel

If you're heading off on vacation and can't take teddy with you, what better place to leave your bear than a hotel in Britain's beautiful West Country. For a small fee your bear will have a comfortable place to stay with three delicious meals a day and even a loving hug at bedtime!

You can even enroll your bears on a range of activities, from visits to the park to storytime sessions and even a trip to an apiary to watch honey "bee"ing made! And, even though your teddies will be having the time of their life, they'll still find time to send you a postcard home to let

you know just how grateful they are for the break.

If your teddy's looking a bit down at heel, you can send him for a health-spa weekend makeover. There he'll be pampered and preened with minor repairs done and an overall clean-up to make him look, and feel, as good as new!

Rikey Austin who owns and runs the teddy bear hotel is an artist by trade and those who are prepared to pay can even have their bear's portrait painted as a lovely gift for when they return from vacation. As Rikey paints, all the bears sit quietly in her studio and watch her at work from their own personal cushions. Rikey is careful to make sure every bear's needs are catered for and she asks their owners to include a list of likes and dislikes so that she can make sure they all remain completely happy during their stay.

Most of the bears that stay at the Withy Hotel are sent by mail – carefully wrapped and marked "special delivery" – but some owners would prefer to bring their bears to Rikey in person – even if it means a ten hour drive!

And, for the most romantic of breaks, your teddies can even get married! The Withy Bears Hotel runs a teddy wedding service for lovestruck bears which for just £14 ($23) includes not only the full wedding service, but a beautiful wedding photo and a marriage certificate to take home and treasure – ahhhh!

For more information you can contact Rikey Austin at

The Withy Bears

117 Staplegrove Road

Taunton,

Somerset

TA1 1DP

Tel – 01823 271 077

Email – Rikey@withybears.freeserve.co.uk

Or visit their website at:
http://www.withybears.freeserve.co.uk

Top Teddies

Jim Humphreys and Leigh Andrews have set up the Cheltenham Teddies' College, offering teds the best education they could ever hope to get. The College boasts 250 students with fees of £250 ($417) a term, that's some going – still, I guess if when ted gets home he's a total brainiac, it'll have been money well spent!

★ *Celebrity Bear* ★
Smokey Bear

Smokey Bear was an important symbol and spokesperson for the United States Forest Service. This responsible fellow was based on a real black bear cub who was rescued from a forest fire and nursed back to health.

Giggly Bear

Why did the elephant sit on the tomato?

He wanted to play squash!

Be Safe Around Bears

Having read *Bear Hugs* you'll of course know how lovely bears are! But, remember, bears are dangerous too.

Left to their own devices they'd never do a soul any harm but as people venture more and more into bear territory, sometimes they can be forced into a position where they feel the need to attack. There is no such thing as a "problem" bear; bears only become "problems" because humans behave irresponsibly. So, if you're planning a vacation in any places where there might be bears, why not follow a few simple rules and make your vacation safe for you – and the bears!

Bears like food! If you're in a cottage or at a campsite make sure you don't leave any tasty-smelling morsels lying around. Bears are natural scavengers and will keep coming back for more as long as the yummy stuff's there.

Garbage counts as food where a bear's concerned. Keep that out of the way and sealed until collection day too.

Camp away from natural paths and streams which bears may use as their routes around their habitat. Camping next to a river makes it hard for a bear to hear you – chances are, if they know you're there, they'll keep away anyway.

If you do encounter a bear – keep calm!

Try to identify what sort of bear it is you're dealing with. In the US and Canada the two likely candidates are the brown (or grizzly) bear or the black bears. If the bear's some distance away and doesn't look particularly interested in you, turn away slowly and go back the way you came.

Don't approach or feed a bear and don't make eye contact.

If a bear follows you . . .

Watch it carefully – but don't look it directly in the eye.

If the bear's aware of you but still a little way away, you can try frightening it off by making yourself look big and talking in a deep, gruff voice.

Continue to back away – remember, don't run, bears are much faster than you'll ever be.

If it's still interested – drop something in your path (not food if you can help it) which will distract its interest – and continue retreating.

If it's a grizzly bear that's following you, you could try climbing a tree – but make sure it's a tall one, you really need to get about 12 feet off the ground.

If a grizzly bear attacks – play dead. Curl in a ball and put your legs against your chest with your head tucked between your knees. Then lace your fingers behind your neck and place your elbows over your knees. Stay still in this position until you're absolutely sure that the bear has moved on.

If a black bear follows you, don't bother climbing a tree – they're great climbers, and you'll be the one that ends up getting stuck.

Black bears that make blowing or snorting noises, swat the ground, or charge you only to veer off at the last moment are acting defensively, so just continue to back away slowly.

If a black bear attacks you. Fight Back! Hit the bear with everything you've got – including sticks and stones and yell in a low gruff voice.

Libearty, Canada suggest you remember the following rhyme.

If the bear is black – fight back

If the bear is brown – fall down

It's doubtful you'll ever have need of any of these techniques if you're a sensible and responsible camper. Most guidebooks have excellent tips on food storage and general safety in bear areas and for more information on being Bear Safe you can contact WSPA Canada at:

WSPA, 44 Victoria St, Suite 1310, Toronto, ON, M5C 1Y2

Tel – 416 369 0044

Email – wspacanada@compuserve.com

Bear Brained

Do you know all there is to know about fearsome and furry critters or are you a bit dim when it comes to the bear essentials? Try this bumper bear quiz to find out:

1. Who did "Teddy" Bears get their name from?

2. What's the proper Inuit name for Polar Bears?

3. A normal bear litter (group of babies) consists of:

A. One to four cubs
B. Six cubs
C. Eight cubs

4. Which so-called bear isn't really a bear at all?

5. Which country is the only place you'll find Pandas in the wild?

6. What's the Indian word for bear?

7. What does "Koala" mean in the Australian Aboriginal language?

8. Which German company is famous for first making teddy bears in Europe?

9. Where does Yogi Bear live?

10. What do koala bears have that's very similar to humans and can get them into trouble with the law?

11. Which Swiss city is famous for its love of bears?

12. Who created Winnie-the-Pooh?

13. Where was Paddington Bear found? (doh!)

14. Bears are:

A. Carnivorous – they survive on a diet of meat.

B. Herbivorous – they survive on a vegetarian diet of leaves, shoots, and berries.

C. Omnivorous – they survive on a diet of

berries, honey, small ground mammals, and fish.

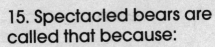

15. Spectacled bears are called that because:

A. Their eyesight isn't very good.

B. They have white-yellow markings around their eyes that look like spectacles.

16. The average life-span of a Giant Panda in the wild is:

A. 10 years

B. 18–20 years

C. 35–40 years

17. The Giant Panda is also know as the:

A. Bamboo Bear

B. Large Bear Cat

C. Black and White Cat-Footed Animal

D. Chinese Panda Bear

E. All of the above

18. What's the biggest part of a Panda's diet?

19. Which major US city has two professional sports teams named after bears?

A. Chicago
B. New York
C. Houston

20. Smokey the Bear was the symbol of the US Forest Service for many years. He was a real bear. What species was he?

21. In the fairy tale *Goldilocks and the Three Bears,* what was wrong with Mama Bear's porridge?

22. Which bear has hairy feet to help it cope in slippery situations?

23. Which is the only bear to be found living in South America?

24. Do Polar Bears live:

A. At the North Pole?
B. At the South Pole?
C. At both poles?

25. Which are the only bear cubs to be born with fur?

A. Brown Bear cubs.
B. Sloth Bear cubs.
C. Polar Bear cubs.

Answers

Give yourself a whacking five points for every right answer – nothing for the wrong one I'm afraid.

13. Paddington Station
12. A. A. Milne
11. Bern
10. Finger prints
9. Jellystone Park
8. Steiff
7. No Drink – koalas get 99 percent of their liquid requirements from the eucalyptus leaves they eat.
6. Baloo
5. China
4. The Koala Bear – it's a marsupial remember. Or, as I'm feeling generous – the Bear Cat, that's not a bear either! Confusing huh?!
3. A. One to four cubs – ahh!
2. Nanook
1. President Theodore "Teddy" Roosevelt

14. C. Omnivorous – they survive on a diet of berries, honey, small ground mammals and fish.

15. B. They have white-yellow markings around their eyes that look like spectacles.

16. B. 18–20

17. E. All of the above. Must be very confusing for them!

18. Bamboo

19. Chicago – they have the Cubs and Da Bears – grrreaaat!

20. American Black Bear

21. It was too cold. (Papa Bear's was too hot, and baby bear's was just right – yum yum!)

22. Polar Bear – their hairy paw pads give them better grip on the ice.

23. Spectacled Bear

24. A. At the North Pole

25. C. Polar Bear cubs – I suppose you'd have to be if you were born at the North Pole – brrr – chilly!

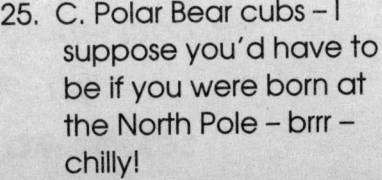

Paw Scores

85–125

Smarter than the Average Bear

You're grrreaaat! Boy do you know your stuff – are you sure you're not actually a bear yourself?! You obviously find animals fascinating and are prepared to take the time to find out all about them. That's a very special thing, as being aware of what animals are like, where they live, and what they need to stay alive is a first step in realizing that conserving their natural habitat and keeping the world safe for them, is a very important thing. You certainly are smarter than the average bear, and believe me, that's pretty darned smart!

45-80

Bear in There

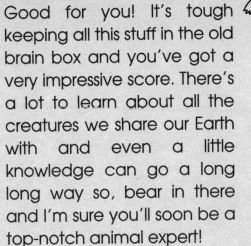

Good for you! It's tough keeping all this stuff in the old brain box and you've got a very impressive score. There's a lot to learn about all the creatures we share our Earth with and even a little knowledge can go a long long way so, bear in there and I'm sure you'll soon be a top-notch animal expert!

0-40

Bearly Awake!

Well you bearly made it I'm afraid! Looks like you snoozed your way through like a dozy koala. Or maybe you were feeling too grizzly to concentrate properly. Well, don't be a bear with a sore head, if you can bear it, paws for thought, start again and I bet we'll bearly be able to stop you getting right to the top of the tree in no time at all!